A Day at the Zoo

Bumblebee Books
London

y Matthew Ruffle Illustrated by Alexandra Abagiu

BUMBLEBEE PAPERBACK EDITION

Illustrations by Alexandra Abagui

A CIP catalogue record for this title is
available from the British Library.

ISBN: 978-1-83934-635-4

Bumblebee Books is an imprint of
Olympia Publishers.

First Published in 2022

Bumblebee Books
Tallis House
2 Tallis Street
London
EC4Y 0AB

Printed in Great Britain

www.olympiapublishers.com

Dedication

Dedicated to Lydia and Harry

I would like to introduce you to Tag and Tilly.
Two fluffy puppies, both incredibly silly.

They get into trouble, whatever they do.
Come on their adventures, you will see this is true.

They both decided on a bright sunny day.
The zoo was the place, they wanted to play.

They packed up some lunch, a drink, and some snacks.
With time getting on, they had better make tracks.

On arrival at the big gates of the zoo.
They were both amazed by the incredible view.

Lions and tigers, giraffes and a bear.
And even orangutans with long flowing hair.

The pups wasted no time, and whilst running around.
Scared a monkey who fell to the ground.

The startled monkey, whose name was Billy.
Wasn't happy and called out to Tilly.

"Lucky for you, that I am OK.
Or the vet would be called, and you'd have to pay."

The dogs bounded on to see what they'd find.
They saw a baboon with a purple behind.
They laughed and they pointed at the baboon's purple bum,
Then Tag shouted out, "It looks like a plum."

Gary the baboon was sad and upset.
Tag and Tilly then filled with regret.
"We're really sorry Gary, for upsetting you so,
accept our apologies, but now we must go."

The final part of the zoo to explore,
Were the sealions, where three of them, sat tall on the shore.

They waited patiently for the crowd to sit down.
Before witnessing, possibly, the best show in town.

The pups sat and watched with amazement and awe.
But Tilly just couldn't resist anymore.
See the keeper had thrown a ball in the water.
Tilly retrieved, like her owner had taught her.

The keeper moved quickly, before grabbing her net.
To retrieve Tilly, now all sopping wet.

To say the least, Tilly’s owners were fuming.

The show had been ruined.
And now Tilly needs grooming.

Now, the puppies' antics had not impressed.
The manager's patience had been put to the test.

He grabbed both the dogs.
And marched back to the start.

Where he ordered the dogs.
That they must depart.

The pups had had fun, but their behaviour that day.
Meant they had both been sent on their way.

Maybe next time, they will learn to be good.
Or maybe, the puppies are just misunderstood.

Acknowledgements

To Deveo Studios.